By Suzy Cato and Kath Bee

Illustrated by

Rose Northey

SCHOLASTIC
AUCKLAND SYDNEY NEW YORK LONDON TORONTO
MEXICO CITY NEW DELHI HONG KONG

For my wonderful Riley, Morgan and Steve who support me in all that I do and are constantly showing me how they "Can Do It", too! — S.C.

For Elsie - always remember, you can do anything — K.B.

To my beautiful Mum, the other storybook singer,
who made their debut in the 90s — R.N.

First published in 2023 by
Scholastic New Zealand Limited
Private Bag 94407, Botany, Auckland 2163,
New Zealand

Scholastic Australia Pty Limited
PO Box 579, Gosford, NSW 2250, Australia

ISBN 978-1-77543-814-4

A catalogue record for this book is available from the National Library of New Zealand.

12 11 10 9 8 7 6 5 4 3 2 1 3 4 5 6 7 8 9/2

Illustrations created in digital paint and collage.
Publishing team: Lynette Evans, Penny Scown and Abby Haverkamp
Designer: Vida Kelly
Typeset in Duper Pro
Printed in China by Toppan Leefung Printing Limited
Scholastic New Zealand's policy is to use papers that are renewable and made efficiently from wood grown in responsibly managed forests, so as to minimise its environmental footprint.

If every great adventure starts
with just one little step,
I'll tie my laces extra-tight and ask,
"Are we there yet?"

If each story that I write begins
with pencil on a page,

I'll join one letter to one more

and take it **stage by stage.**

I don't have to BE the best,
I just need to be MY best!
And once I start, I'll keep on going
and encourage all the rest.

If all I need to do to **dance**
is get up on the floor,

I'll give a **wiggle**, give a **shake**,
and then **shout out** for more!

If I get the urge to **sing**,
I'll open up my mouth.

I'll sing **LOUD**
and I'll be **PROUD** ...

of whatever sound
comes out!

MoOOOOOoo

I don't have to BE the best,
I just need to be MY best!
And once I start, I'll keep on going
and encourage all the rest.

I can do it! I can do it! I can do it!
There's always someone there
to help me through it.
I can do it! I can do it!

If all I need to do to understand
is question why,

I'll **ask** ...

and **ask** again ...

until I'm **satisfied.**

If all I need to do to find a friend is say hello,
I'll be **brave** and **share a smile**
and let our friendship grow.

I don't have to BE the best,
I just need to be MY best!
And once I start, I'll keep on going
and encourage all the rest.

I can do it! I can do it! I can do it!
There's always someone there
to help me through it.
I can do it! I can do it!

And if I get knocked down,
I'll get back up again,
because this thing called life
is like a roller coaster ride,

and I **know** deep down inside ...

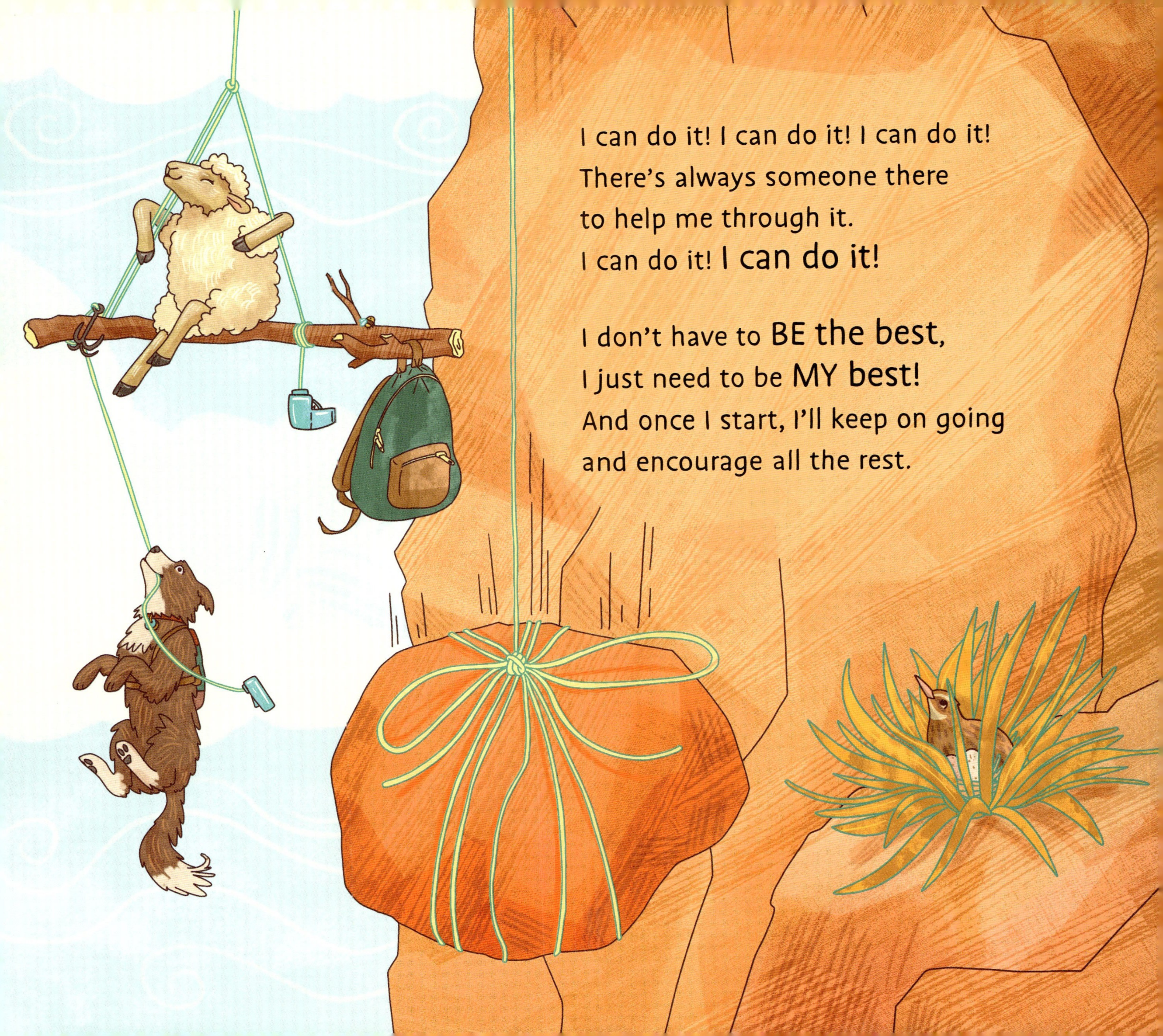

I can do it! I can do it! I can do it!
There's always someone there
to help me through it.
I can do it! I can do it!

I don't have to BE the best,
I just need to be MY best!
And once I start, I'll keep on going
and encourage all the rest.

I can do it! I can do it! I can do it!
There's always someone there
to help me through it.
I can do it! I can do it!
I CAN DO IT!